Claude was a dog. Claude was a small dog.
Claude was a small, plump dog.

Claude was a small, plump dog who liked
wearing a beret and a lovely red jumper.

Claude lived with his owners Mr and Mrs Shinyshoes
and his best friend Sir Bobblysock.

Every day, when Mr and Mrs Shinyshoes went out to work,
Claude and Sir Bobblysock would get ready to have an
adventure.

Where will they go today?

To GEORGIA,
THOMAS, EUAN
and CONNOR

Thank you
to my friend
CHARLOTTE REED,
the original
Giddy Kipper

HODDER CHILDREN'S BOOKS

First published in Great Britain in 2016
by Hodder and Stoughton
This edition published in 2017

Text and illustrations © Alex T. Smith 2016

The moral rights of the
author/illustrator have been asserted.

A CIP catalogue record of this book
is available from the British Library.

ISBN: 9781 444 90368 3

10 9 8 7 6 5 4 3 2 1

Printed and bound in China.

Hodder Children's Books
An imprint of
Hachette Children's Group
Part of Hodder and Stoughton
Carmelite House
50 Victoria Embankment
London EC4Y 0DZ

An Hachette UK Company
www.hachette.co.uk

www.hachettechildrens.co.uk

Hodder
Children's
Books

FSC
www.fsc.org
MIX
Paper from
responsible sources
FSC® C104740

CLAUDE

All at Sea

Alex T. Smith

One day, Claude had been painting
and now he needed a bath.

Sir Bobblysock said so, and he
knew ALL about these things.

So Claude stashed his paintbrushes in his beret and turned on the taps in the bathroom. Then he went to find his bath toys.

Downstairs, Sir Bobblysock busied himself with his knick-knacks.

Nobody
remembered the water until...

DRIP!

DRIP!

DRIP!

BATHROOM

...it was too late.

WHOOOSH!

went the water.

'Yikes!' went Claude, and he grabbed Sir Bobblysock and **leapt** into the bathtub as a huge **wave** carried them

down
the
stairs...

along the street...

and into the
deep blue sea.

SPLASH!

Claude had **never** sailed a bathtub on the ocean before.

It was **very** wet and **stonking** good fun!

Whilst Claude looked at all the splashy water,
Sir Bobbysock busied himself reading some signs.

They seemed to be **jolly important**
and all about someone called Nigel.

'I wonder who Nigel is?' said Claude.

But before Sir Bobblysock could tell him...

...a GIGANTIC
sea monster
(called Nigel)

suddenly appeared and...

GOBBLED

them up!

It was very dark and very damp in Nigel's tummy.

Claude was getting a bit scared and

Sir Bobblysock's stitches started to quiver

when voices came from the darkness...

'Can you help us, Claude?' cried Captain Poopdeck.

'We're **stuck!**' squawked Barry the seagull.

'We must escape!' shouted Cindy Seaweed.

Claude LOVED helping, so he hopped on board
Captain Poopdeck's boat. He emptied his beret out
to see if he had anything useful in there.

He did.

First, they tried the stepladder.
But that didn't work. It was too short.

'We could climb out using the rope!'
said Cindy. It was a **very** good idea,
but that didn't work either because
it was in such a

t a n g l e.

The Giddy Kipper

'This is a **disaster**,'
cried Captain Poopdeck.

'We're **trapped**!'
gasped Cindy Seaweed.

'We are going to be stuck in here
for ever!' yelped Sir Bobblysock.

'**And ever**!' said Barry, helpfully.

Sir Bobblysock's knees knocked
and he started to hiccup.
Suddenly Claude had a
wonderful idea...

'If we give Nigel the hiccups, we might fly
out and not be stuck in here any more?'

Everyone thought this was a super idea, so they all

grabbed a brush and started tickling...

Out on the ocean,
Nigel's tummy started
to **twitch**,
and **wiggle**,
and **jiggle** until...

HICCUP!

Everyone flew out.

'Oh dear!' said Nigel,

'I didn't mean to gobble you all up.
I don't usually eat
seagulls or people
or dogs or socks.
I much prefer
Seaweed Sandwiches.
The problem is, I just can't
see very well.'

Claude wagged his tail. He could do some more helping!

He quickly reached into his beret and handed
Nigel the enormous glasses he'd found
in there earlier.

'Thank you!' said Nigel. 'Now I'll never gobble up anyone ever again!'

'HOORAY FOR CLAUDE!' everyone shouted.

By now, it was getting late, and Claude and Sir Bobblysock had to get home, so they said goodbye to their new friends and promised to come back and play next bathtime.

When Mr and Mrs Shinyshoes came home, they couldn't understand why their bath was in the kitchen.

'Do you think Claude knows anything about this?' said Mrs Shinyshoes.

'Let's ask him when he wakes up!'
said Mr Shinyshoes.

Claude smiled a little smile. Of course he knew why their bath was in the kitchen. And we do too, don't we?

THE END.